Welcome to Saddleback's *Illustrated Classics*™

We are proud to welcome you to Saddleback's *Illustrated Classics*™. Saddleback's *Illustrated Classics*™ was designed specifically for the classroom to introduce readers to many of the great classics in literature. Each text, written and adapted by teachers and researchers, has been edited using the Dale-Chall vocabulary system. In addition, much time and effort has been spent to ensure that these high-interest stories retain all of the excitement, intrigue, and adventure of the original books.

With these graphically *Illustrated Classics*™, you learn what happens in the story in a number of different ways. One way is by reading the words a character says. Another way is by looking at the drawings of the character. The artist can tell you what kind of person a character is and what he or she is thinking or feeling.

This series will help you to develop confidence and a sense of accomplishment as you finish each novel. The stories in Saddleback's *Illustrated Classics*™ are fun to read. And remember, fun motivates!

Overview

Everyone deserves to read the best literature our language has to offer. Saddleback's *Illustrated Classics*™ was designed to acquaint readers with the most famous stories from the world's greatest authors, while teaching essential skills. You will learn how to:

- Establish a purpose for reading
- Activate prior knowledge
- Evaluate your reading
- Listen to the language as it is written
- Extend literary and language appreciation through discussion and writing activities.

Reading is one of the most important skills you will ever learn. It provides the key to all kinds of information. By reading the *Illustrated Classics*™, you will develop confidence and the self-satisfaction that comes from accomplishment—a solid foundation for any reader.

Remember,

"Today's readers are tomorrow's leaders."

William Shakespeare

William Shakespeare was baptized on April 26, 1564, in Stratford-on-Avon, England, the third child of John Shakespeare, a well-to-do merchant, and Mary Arden, his wife. Young William probably attended the Stratford grammar school, where he learned English, Greek, and a great deal of Latin. Historians aren't sure of the exact date of Shakespeare's birth.

In 1582, Shakespeare married Anne Hathaway. By 1583 the couple had a daughter, Susanna, and two years later the twins, Hamnet and Judith. Somewhere between 1585 and 1592 Shakespeare went to London, where he became first an actor and then a playwright. His acting company, *The King's Men*, appeared most often in the *Globe* theater, a part of which Shakespeare himself owned.

In all, Shakespeare is believed to have written thirty-seven plays, several nondramatic poems, and a number of sonnets. In 1611 when he left the active life of the theater, he returned to Stratford and became a country gentleman, living in the second-largest house in town. For five years he lived a quiet life. Then, on April 23, 1616, William Shakespeare died and was buried in Trinity Church in Stratford. From his own time to the present, Shakespeare is considered one of the greatest writers of the English-speaking world.

William Shakespeare

Julius Caesar

BRUTUS

MARK ANTONY

JULIUS CAESAR

CASSIUS

CALPURNIA

CASCA

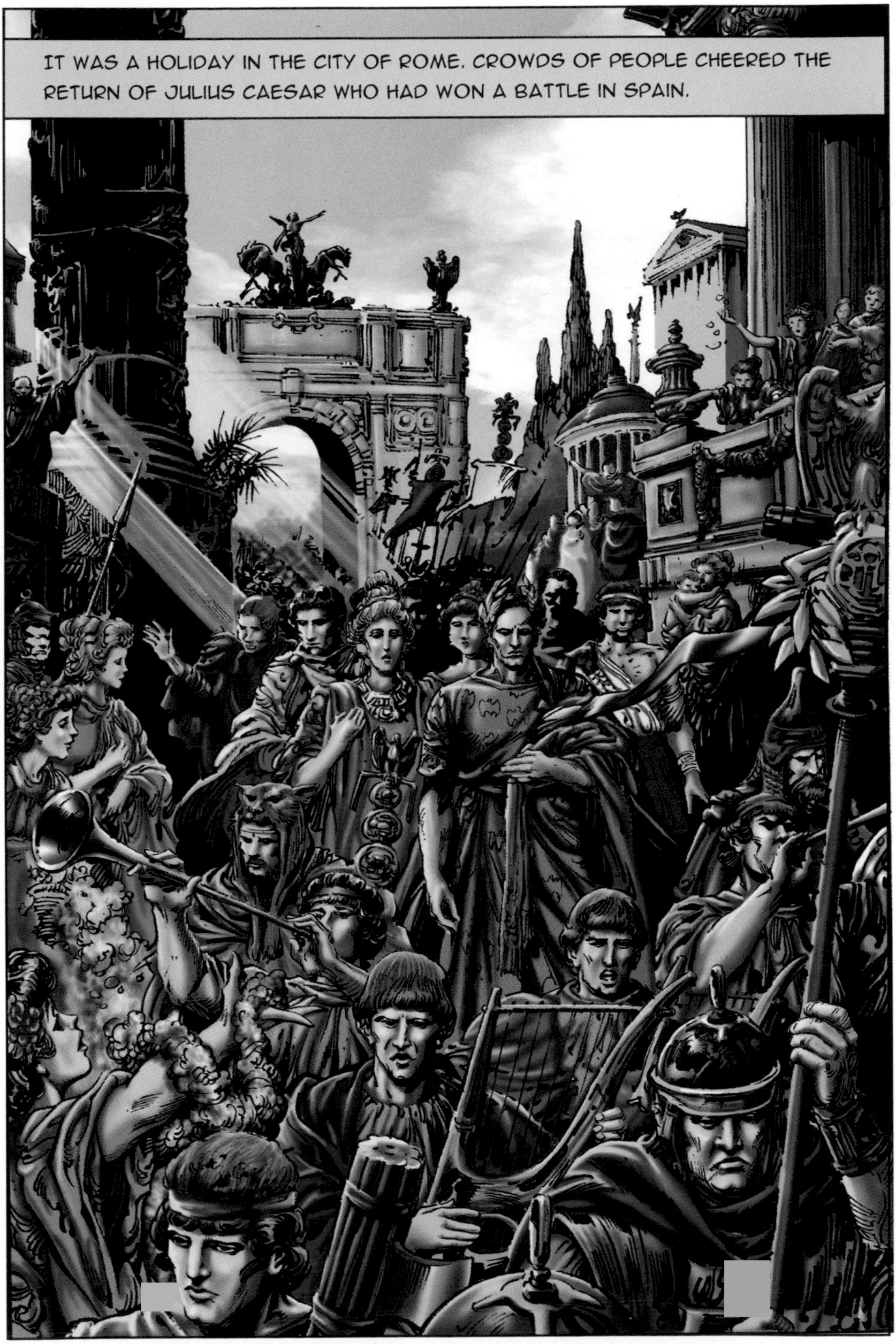
IT WAS A HOLIDAY IN THE CITY OF ROME. CROWDS OF PEOPLE CHEERED THE RETURN OF JULIUS CAESAR WHO HAD WON A BATTLE IN SPAIN.

BUT NOT EVERYONE WAS HAPPY. TWO GOVERNMENT OFFICIALS,* FLAVIUS AND MARULLUS, TRIED TO SEND AWAY SOME OF THE CROWDS.

GO HOME YOU LAZY MEN!

WHY ARE YOU HERE IN HOLIDAY CLOTHES INSTEAD OF WORKING IN YOUR SHOPS?

WHY, SIR . . . I AM A GOOD SHOEMAKER! BUT TODAY I CAME OUT TO SEE CAESAR AND CELEBRATE WITH HIM.

FOR SHAME! HE DID NOT FIGHT A FOREIGN** ENEMY, BUT THE SONS OF A GREAT ROMAN— POMPEY.

POMPEY, WHO FOUGHT TO KEEP CAESAR FROM MAKING HIMSELF RULER OF ROME! POMPEY, WHOM YOU HAVE OFTEN CHEERED FOR IN THESE VERY STREETS!

HOW MANY TIMES HAVE YOU WAITED ALL DAY JUST TO CHEER POMPEY AS HE PASSED BY? NOW YOU DRESS UP TO CHEER THE MAN WHO SHED POMPEY'S BLOOD!

* those whose jobs involve the running of a city, state, or country

** from another country

THAT DAY HAP-
PENED TO BE A
YEARLY HOLIDAY TO
HONOR THE GOD
LUPERCUS.* THERE
WAS TO BE A FOOT
RACE, AND PEOPLE
HAD DECORATED
ALL THE STATUES IN
THE CITY.

WE MUST REMOVE THESE DECORATIONS. THEY ARE AN INSULT TO THE MEMORY OF POMPEY!

ARE WE ALLOWED TO DO THAT? AFTER ALL IT *IS* THE FEAST OF LUPERCAL!

WE DON'T NEED SUCH THINGS TO REMIND US OF WHAT CAESAR HAS DONE. BEFORE WE KNOW IT, HE WILL MAKE HIMSELF KING!

YOU GO THAT WAY. . . I'LL GO THIS WAY. REMOVE ANY OF CAESAR'S DECORATIONS THAT YOU SEE.

I'LL DO IT!

* a god who would bless the fields with good crops

* The Roman month was divided into the kalends, the ides, and the nones; in March the ides fell on the 15th.

* someone who predicts the future from signs and omens

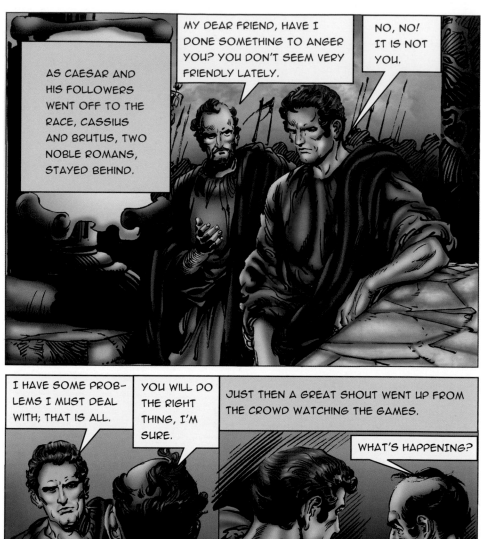

AS CAESAR AND HIS FOLLOWERS WENT OFF TO THE RACE, CASSIUS AND BRUTUS, TWO NOBLE ROMANS, STAYED BEHIND.

MY DEAR FRIEND, HAVE I DONE SOMETHING TO ANGER YOU? YOU DON'T SEEM VERY FRIENDLY LATELY.

NO, NO! IT IS NOT YOU.

I HAVE SOME PROBLEMS I MUST DEAL WITH; THAT IS ALL.

YOU WILL DO THE RIGHT THING, I'M SURE.

JUST THEN A GREAT SHOUT WENT UP FROM THE CROWD WATCHING THE GAMES.

WHAT'S HAPPENING?

I'M AFRAID THE PEOPLE ARE CHOOSING CAESAR TO BE THEIR KING!

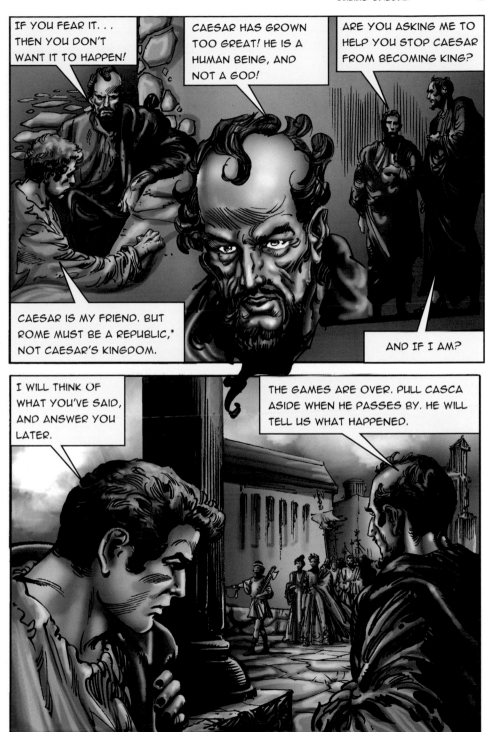

* a government ruled by the people

MEANWHILE, CAESAR AND HIS FOLLOWERS ARRIVED AT THE PLACE WHERE BRUTUS AND CASSIUS WERE TALKING.

I DON'T LIKE THE LOOKS OF THAT CASSIUS.

DON'T FEAR HIM, CAESAR. HE'S NOT DANGEROUS.

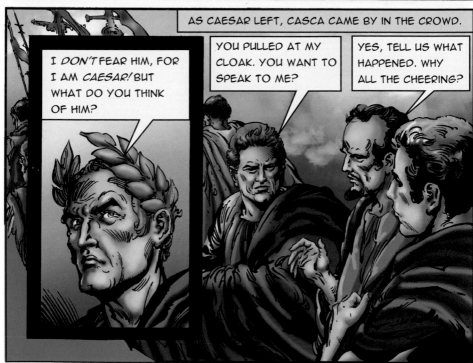

AS CAESAR LEFT, CASCA CAME BY IN THE CROWD.

I *DON'T* FEAR HIM, FOR I AM *CAESAR!* BUT WHAT DO YOU THINK OF HIM?

YOU PULLED AT MY CLOAK. YOU WANT TO SPEAK TO ME?

YES, TELL US WHAT HAPPENED. WHY ALL THE CHEERING?

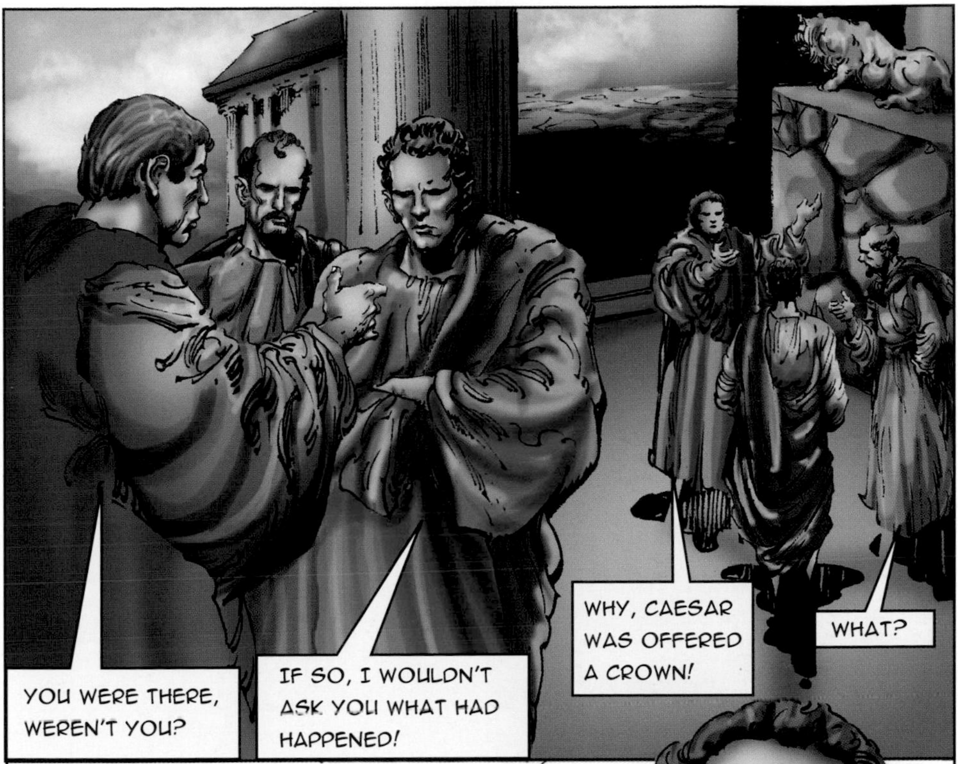
YOU WERE THERE, WEREN'T YOU?
IF SO, I WOULDN'T ASK YOU WHAT HAD HAPPENED!
WHY, CAESAR WAS OFFERED A CROWN!
WHAT?

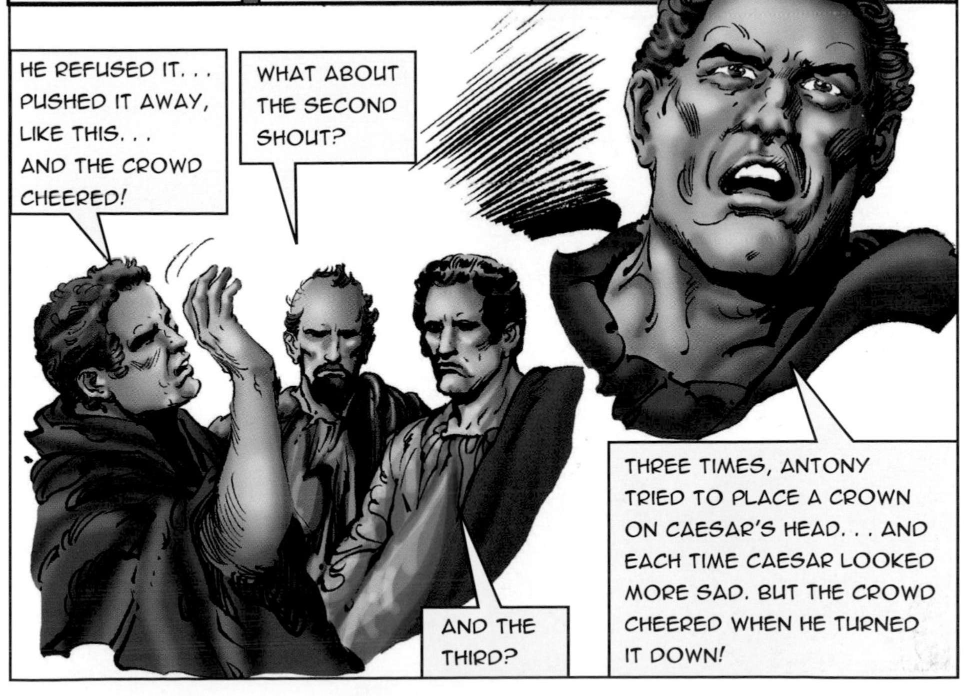
HE REFUSED IT. . . PUSHED IT AWAY, LIKE THIS. . . AND THE CROWD CHEERED!
WHAT ABOUT THE SECOND SHOUT?
AND THE THIRD?
THREE TIMES, ANTONY TRIED TO PLACE A CROWN ON CAESAR'S HEAD. . . AND EACH TIME CAESAR LOOKED MORE SAD. BUT THE CROWD CHEERED WHEN HE TURNED IT DOWN!

THE PEOPLE LOVE HIM AS A DICTATOR,* BUT THEY ARE NOT YET READY TO ACCEPT HIM AS A KING.

BY THE WAY, CASCA, WILL YOU DINE WITH ME TOMORROW?

IF I STILL LIVE. . . AND YOUR DINNER IS WORTH EATING! FOR NOW, FAREWELL.

IF YOU WISH TO TALK TO ME PRIVATELY, COME TOMORROW. I'LL WAIT AT HOME FOR YOU.

GOOD! I'LL BE THERE.

SO BRUTUS LEFT, AND CASSIUS STOOD ALONE.

TONIGHT. . . I WILL SEE THAT LETTERS ARE TOSSED THROUGH BRUTUS' WINDOW.

THEY'LL SEEM TO BE FROM LEADING CITIZENS** HINTING THAT CAESAR WILL MAKE HIMSELF KING. I'LL HAVE BRUTUS ON MY SIDE YET!

* a leader given full power in times of trouble

** members of a city or country who have the right to vote

THAT NIGHT A TERRIBLE STORM RAGED, BUT CASCA WAS OUT IN IT.

NEVER TILL TONIGHT HAVE I SEEN A STORM DROPPING SUCH FIRE ON US!

A LION. . . BUT HE IS TOO FRIGHTENED TO ATTACK ME!

IT IS A SIGN FROM THE GODS! THEY ARE ANGRY WITH THE MEN OF ROME!

* knew by seeing or hearing
** rulers who refuse to follow the law and often treat their people harshly

I HEAR THE SENATORS* PLAN TO MAKE CAESAR KING TOMORROW!

THE ROMAN PEOPLE ARE WEAKER THAN I THOUGHT IF THEY NEED A *KING* TO RULE THEM.

BUT PERHAPS YOU SERVE CAESAR GLADLY! IF SO, I AM READY TO DEFEND MYSELF!

NO, NO! I FEEL AS YOU DO! AND I WILL JOIN YOU IF YOU HAVE A PLAN AGAINST HIM.

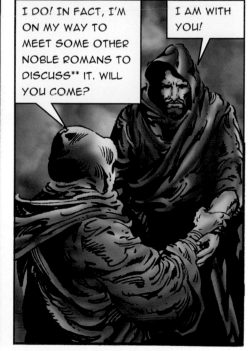

I DO! IN FACT, I'M ON MY WAY TO MEET SOME OTHER NOBLE ROMANS TO DISCUSS** IT. WILL YOU COME?

I AM WITH YOU!

* men who are elected to help rule a city or a country

** talk over

BUT WAIT! HERE COMES SOMEONE!

IT IS CINNA. HE IS ONE OF US!

I CAME TO FIND YOU! WE ARE WAITING AT THE MEETING PLACE!

IF YOU COULD ONLY WIN BRUTUS TO OUR SIDE! ALL THE PEOPLE LOVE HIM AND BELIEVE IN HIM.

HE THINKS AS WE DO, CINNA. I AM SURE HE WILL JOIN US SOON.

THESE LETTERS WILL HELP PERSUADE* HIM. TOSS ONE IN AT HIS WINDOW, THE OTHERS WHERE ONLY *HE* CAN FIND THEM.

ALL RIGHT. I WILL MEET YOU LATER.

COME CASCA. BEFORE IT IS DAY, WE SHALL SEE BRUTUS AT HIS HOUSE. BY THEN HE WILL BE ONE OF US!

*urge or encourage someone to believe or to do something

AT THAT VERY HOUR, BRUTUS WAS WALKING IN HIS GARDEN. HE COULD NOT SLEEP.

LUCIUS, WAKE UP! COME HERE!

YOU CALLED, SIR?

TAKE A CANDLE INTO MY STUDY, LUCIUS. WHEN IT IS LIGHTED, COME AND CALL ME.

I WILL, SIR.

ALONE AGAIN, BRUTUS TRIED TO SORT OUT HIS THOUGHTS.

CAESAR CAN BE STOPPED ONLY BY DEATH. BUT IS IT RIGHT TO KILL HIM?

THE CANDLE IS LIGHTED. AND IN YOUR STUDY, NEAR THE WINDOW, I FOUND THIS.

* members of one's family who lived long ago
** Tarquinius Superbus, the last king of Rome, who was driven from the city by his people

JUST THEN, THE SERVANT LUCIUS RETURNED.

YOU ARE RIGHT, SIR. IT *IS* THE FIFTEENTH OF MARCH.

GOOD. NOW GO TO THE GATE. SOMEONE'S KNOCKING.

SIR, IT IS YOUR FRIEND CASSIUS. . . AND SOME OTHER MEN I COULD NOT SEE.

LET THEM COME IN.

GOOD DAY! DO WE WAKE YOU?

NO. I'VE BEEN AWAKE ALL NIGHT. DO I KNOW THESE MEN?

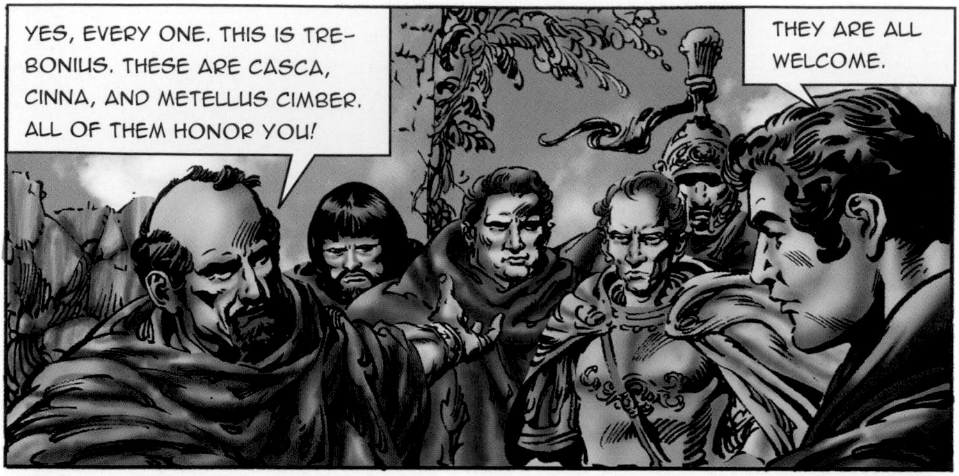
YES, EVERY ONE. THIS IS TREBONIUS. THESE ARE CASCA, CINNA, AND METELLUS CIMBER. ALL OF THEM HONOR YOU!
THEY ARE ALL WELCOME.

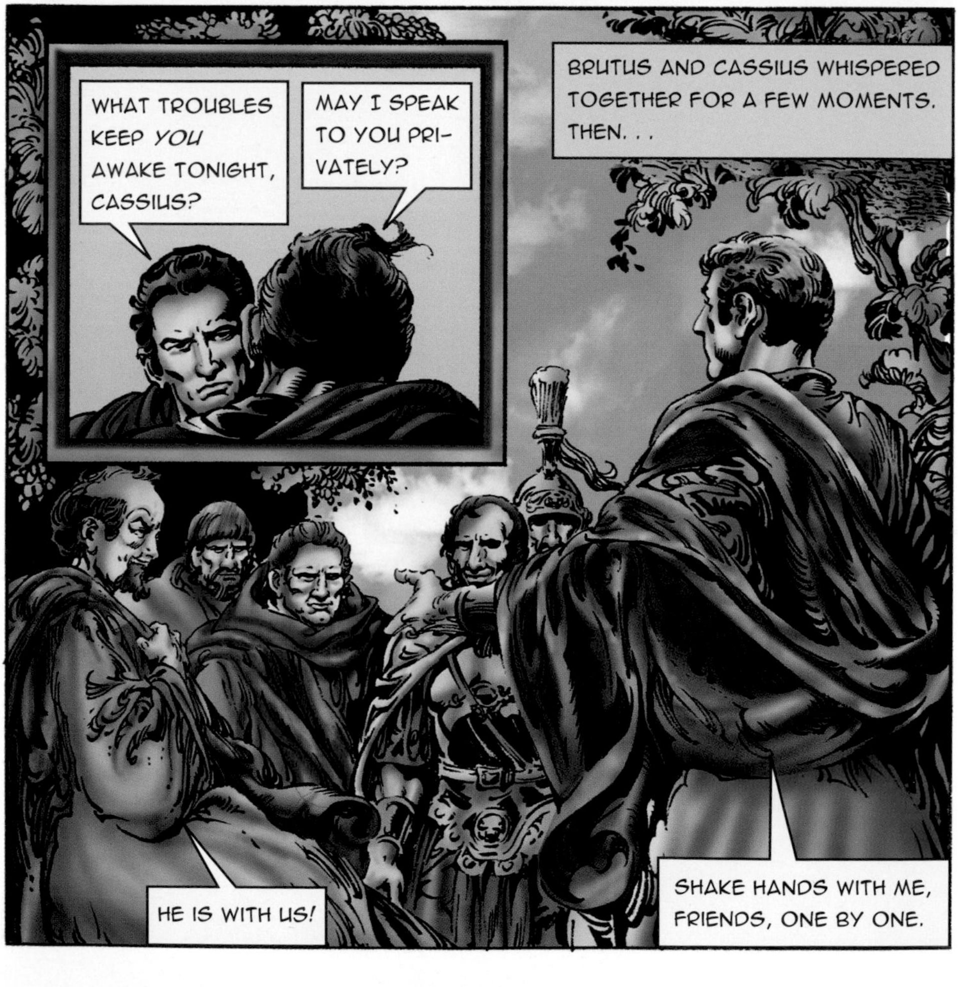
WHAT TROUBLES KEEP *YOU* AWAKE TONIGHT, CASSIUS?
MAY I SPEAK TO YOU PRIVATELY?
BRUTUS AND CASSIUS WHISPERED TOGETHER FOR A FEW MOMENTS. THEN. . .
SHAKE HANDS WITH ME, FRIENDS, ONE BY ONE.
HE IS WITH US!

YES, WE WILL SWEAR TO CARRY OUT OUR PLAN!

NO, NOT AN OATH!*

OUR HONEST WORD, HONESTLY GIVEN, IS ENOUGH FOR ANY TRUE ROMAN.

SHALL NO MAN BE TOUCHED BUT CAESAR?

A GOOD POINT. I THINK MARK ANTONY SHOULD DIE TOO!

NO, NO!

WE ARE NOT BUTCHERS! WE DON'T KILL IN ANGER. WE ACT FOR THE GOOD OF ALL.

BESIDES, MARK ANTONY CAN DO NO MORE TO HURT US THAN CAESAR'S *ARM* COULD, IF HIS HEAD WERE CUT OFF!

* a very solemn or serious promise

LISTEN! THE CLOCK STRIKES THREE.

IT IS TIME WE LEFT.

BUT SUPPOSE CAESAR DOES NOT GO TO THE CAPITOL TODAY? THE OMENS* ARE BAD, AND HE HAS BECOME VERY SUPERSTITIOUS.**

DON'T WORRY, I KNOW WHAT TO DO. I'LL GET HIM TO THE CAPITOL.

THEN WE WILL MEET BY EIGHT O'CLOCK.

AGREED! WE'LL ALL BE THERE. GOODBYE, BRUTUS.

* mysterious signs that are supposed to warn of future events
** believing in all sorts of supernatural signs

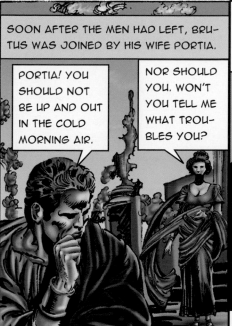

SOON AFTER THE MEN HAD LEFT, BRU-TUS WAS JOINED BY HIS WIFE PORTIA.

PORTIA! YOU SHOULD NOT BE UP AND OUT IN THE COLD MORNING AIR.

NOR SHOULD YOU. WON'T YOU TELL ME WHAT TROU-BLES YOU?

ALL NIGHT YOU HAVE WALKED AND SIGHED. EARLIER, WHEN I ASKED WHAT TROUBLED YOU, YOU WERE CROSS WITH ME.

IT IS ONLY THAT I AM NOT FEELING WELL!

DON'T KNEEL, DEAR PORTIA!

I WOULDN'T HAVE TO, IF YOU WOULD KEEP YOUR MARRIAGE VOWS.

AM I ONLY SOMEONE TO FIX YOUR MEALS AND SHARE YOUR BED. . . OR AM I TRULY YOUR WIFE, A PART OF YOU, TO SHARE YOUR SECRETS?

YOU'RE MY TRUE WIFE, AS DEAR TO ME AS MY HEART'S BLOOD!

I AM LOYAL, BRUTUS, AND I CAN KEEP YOUR SECRETS!

MY DEAR LOVE, I WILL TELL YOU EVERYTHING!

BUT WAIT. . . SOMEONE'S AT THE GATE! GO INSIDE QUICKLY, AND WE'LL SPEAK LATER.

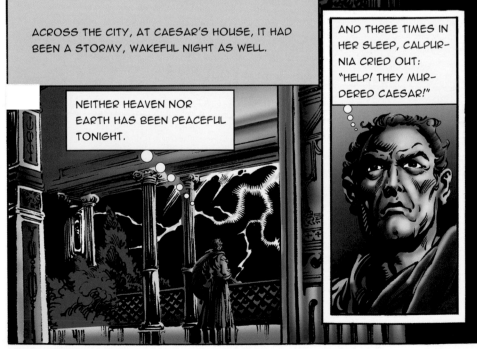

ACROSS THE CITY, AT CAESAR'S HOUSE, IT HAD BEEN A STORMY, WAKEFUL NIGHT AS WELL.

NEITHER HEAVEN NOR EARTH HAS BEEN PEACEFUL TONIGHT.

AND THREE TIMES IN HER SLEEP, CALPURNIA CRIED OUT: "HELP! THEY MURDERED CAESAR!"

TROUBLED, CAESAR CALLED A SERVANT TO HIS SIDE.

GO AND TELL THE PRIESTS TO MAKE SACRIFICES*, AND LET ME KNOW WHAT THEY SAY.

AT ONCE, SIR.

AS THE SERVANT HURRIED AWAY, CAESAR'S WIFE CALPURNIA CAME INTO THE ROOM.

CAESAR! YOU MUST NOT GO OUT OF THE HOUSE TODAY!

I'VE NEVER BELIEVED IN SIGNS AND OMENS. . . BUT AWFUL THINGS HAVE BEEN SEEN DURING THE NIGHT.

GHOST-SOLDIERS FOUGHT IN THE CLOUDS, DEAD MEN LEFT THEIR GRAVES, SPIRITS SCREAMED IN THE STREETS. I'M AFRAID!

THESE SIGNS ARE FOR EVERYONE, NOT JUST FOR ME. I AM NOT AFRAID. DEATH WILL COME WHEN IT WILL COME!

* offerings to the gods

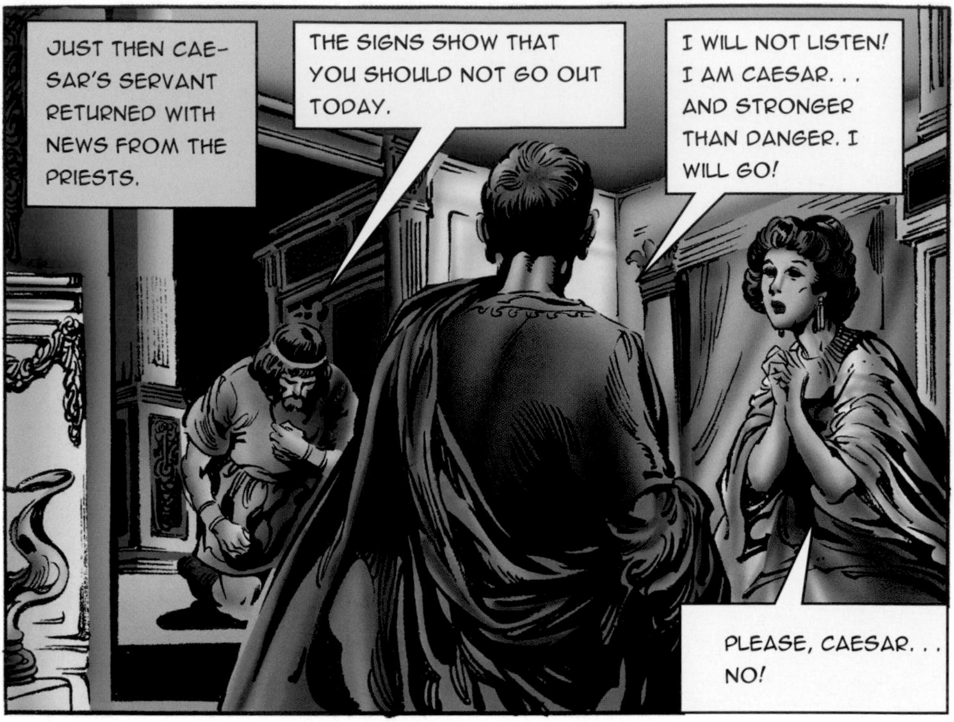
JUST THEN CAESAR'S SERVANT RETURNED WITH NEWS FROM THE PRIESTS.
THE SIGNS SHOW THAT YOU SHOULD NOT GO OUT TODAY.
I WILL NOT LISTEN! I AM CAESAR. . . AND STRONGER THAN DANGER. I WILL GO!
PLEASE, CAESAR. . . NO!

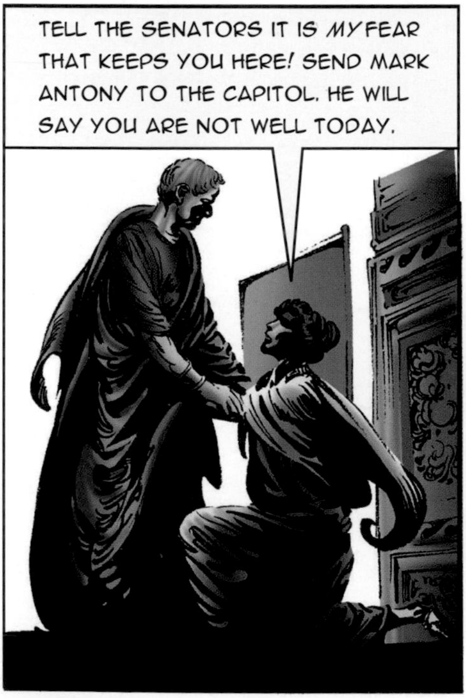
TELL THE SENATORS IT IS *MY* FEAR THAT KEEPS YOU HERE! SEND MARK ANTONY TO THE CAPITOL. HE WILL SAY YOU ARE NOT WELL TODAY.

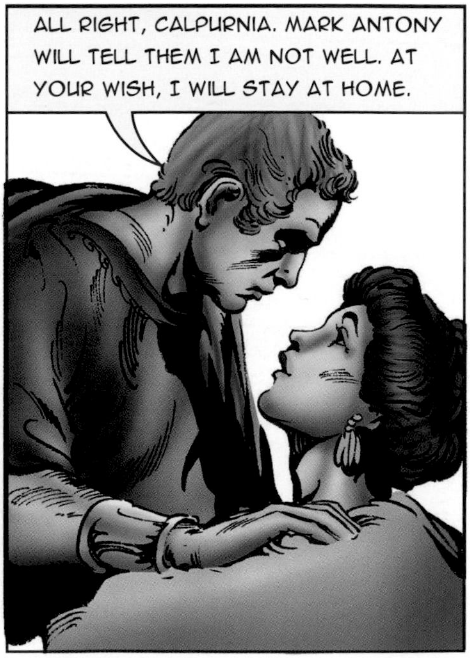
ALL RIGHT, CALPURNIA. MARK ANTONY WILL TELL THEM I AM NOT WELL. AT YOUR WISH, I WILL STAY AT HOME.

JUST THEN DECIUS ARRIVED. . . THE PLOTTER* WHO HAD SAID HE WOULD SEE TO IT THAT CAESAR CAME TO THE CAPITOL.

GOOD DAY, CAESAR! I'VE COME TO TAKE YOU TO THE CAPITOL.

YOU ARE JUST IN TIME TO TAKE A MESSAGE TO THE SENATORS. I WILL NOT COME TODAY.

SAY HE IS SICK.

NO, NO. I HAVE NO NEED TO LIE.

SIMPLY TELL THEM I WILL NOT COME. THAT IS ENOUGH.

BUT BECAUSE YOU ARE MY FRIEND, I WILL TELL YOU THE REAL REASON. IT IS CALPURNIA, MY WIFE, WHO KEEPS ME AT HOME.

I HAD SUCH TERRIBLE DREAMS LAST NIGHT!

* someone who plans evil

I SAW CAESAR'S STATUE, LIKE A FOUNTAIN, SPOUTING BLOOD. AND MANY ROMANS CAME SMILING, AND WASHED THEIR HANDS IN IT!

SHE HAS BEGGED ME ON HER KNEES TO STAY AT HOME TODAY.

HER DREAM IS RIGHT, CAESAR, BUT YOU HAVE NOT UNDERSTOOD IT CORRECTLY!

YOUR STATUE SPOUTING BLOOD MEANS THAT ROME WILL RECEIVE STRENGTH AND GREATNESS FROM YOU. *THAT* IS WHAT THE DREAM MEANS!

YOU SEE, THE SENATORS PLAN TO GIVE YOU A CROWN TODAY! IF YOU DO NOT COME, THEY MAY CHANGE THEIR MINDS.

SOME WILL LAUGH, AND SAY, "WAIT UNTIL ANOTHER TIME WHEN CAESAR'S WIFE HAS BETTER DREAMS!"

THEY'LL WHISPER, "THE MIGHTY CAESAR IS AFRAID."

YOU MAKE CALPURNIA'S FEAR SEEM FOOLISH.

I AM ASHAMED THAT I AGREED WITH HER. I WILL GO! BRING ME MY ROBE.

THEN, AS CAESAR GOT READY, OTHERS ARRIVED.

HERE IS PUBLIUS, COMING TO WALK WITH ME. AND BRUTUS!

GOOD DAY, CAESAR!

WELCOME, PUBLIUS! AND YOU, BRUTUS, YOU'RE OUT EARLY. CASCA, CAIUS LIGARIUS... COME IN!

AND HERE'S ANTONY—UP EARLY EVEN AFTER A NIGHT OF MERRY-MAKING!

DEAR FRIENDS, THANK YOU FOR COM-ING! HAVE SOME WINE, AND WE'LL ALL GO TO THE CAPITOL TOGETHER.

AS THE PLOTTERS WAITED TO GO WITH CAESAR TO THE SENATE,* OTHER PEOPLE WERE TRYING TO FIND WAYS TO WARN HIM.

ONE OF THESE WAS ARTEMIDORUS.

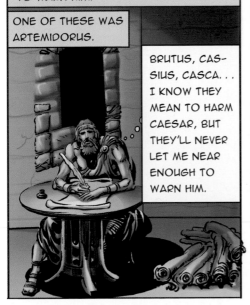

BRUTUS, CASSIUS, CASCA... I KNOW THEY MEAN TO HARM CAESAR, BUT THEY'LL NEVER LET ME NEAR ENOUGH TO WARN HIM.

I'LL WRITE A NOTE AND TRY TO GIVE IT TO CAESAR AS HE PASSES. IF HE READS IT, HE MAY YET LIVE!

ANOTHER WAS THE OLD SOOTHSAYER WHO HAD WARNED CAESAR ABOUT THE IDES OF MARCH.

I SEE GREAT HARM COMING TO CAESAR. I MUST WARN HIM AGAIN TO TAKE CARE!

I MUST FIND A PLACE HE WILL PASS ON HIS WAY. I WILL SPEAK TO HIM ONCE MORE!

* the building in which the senators met for government business; the Capitol

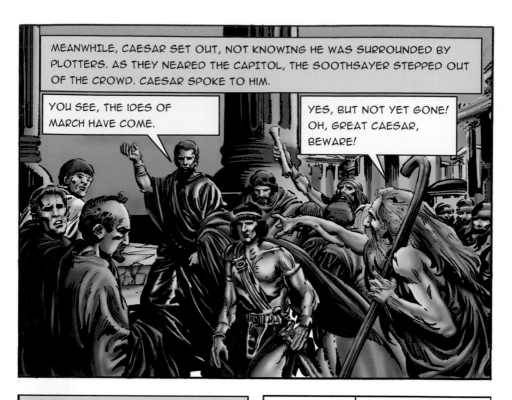

MEANWHILE, CAESAR SET OUT, NOT KNOWING HE WAS SURROUNDED BY PLOTTERS. AS THEY NEARED THE CAPITOL, THE SOOTHSAYER STEPPED OUT OF THE CROWD. CAESAR SPOKE TO HIM.

YOU SEE, THE IDES OF MARCH HAVE COME.

YES, BUT NOT YET GONE! OH, GREAT CAESAR, BEWARE!

THEN ARTEMIDORUS RUSHED UP TO CAESAR.

HAIL, CAESAR! PLEASE READ THIS PETITION,* I BEG YOU!

THIS IS NOT THE TIME FOR SUCH THINGS.

BUT THIS CONCERNS YOU, AND NOW!

ALL THE MORE REASON TO WAIT. I MUST PUT THE PEOPLE'S BUSINESS BEFORE MY OWN.

* a paper asking for a favor

SO, CAESAR MOVED ON TO THE CAPITOL, NEVER THINKING OF DANGER. BUT SOME OF THE PLOTTERS WERE NERVOUS.*

LOOK! IS POPILIUS WARNING CAESAR OF OUR PLOT?

DON'T WORRY! CAESAR IS STILL SMILING.

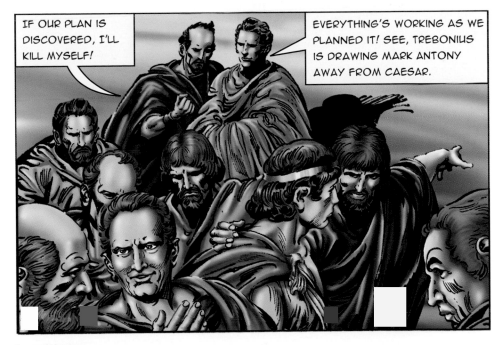

IF OUR PLAN IS DISCOVERED, I'LL KILL MYSELF!

EVERYTHING'S WORKING AS WE PLANNED IT! SEE, TREBONIUS IS DRAWING MARK ANTONY AWAY FROM CAESAR.

* upset, jumpy

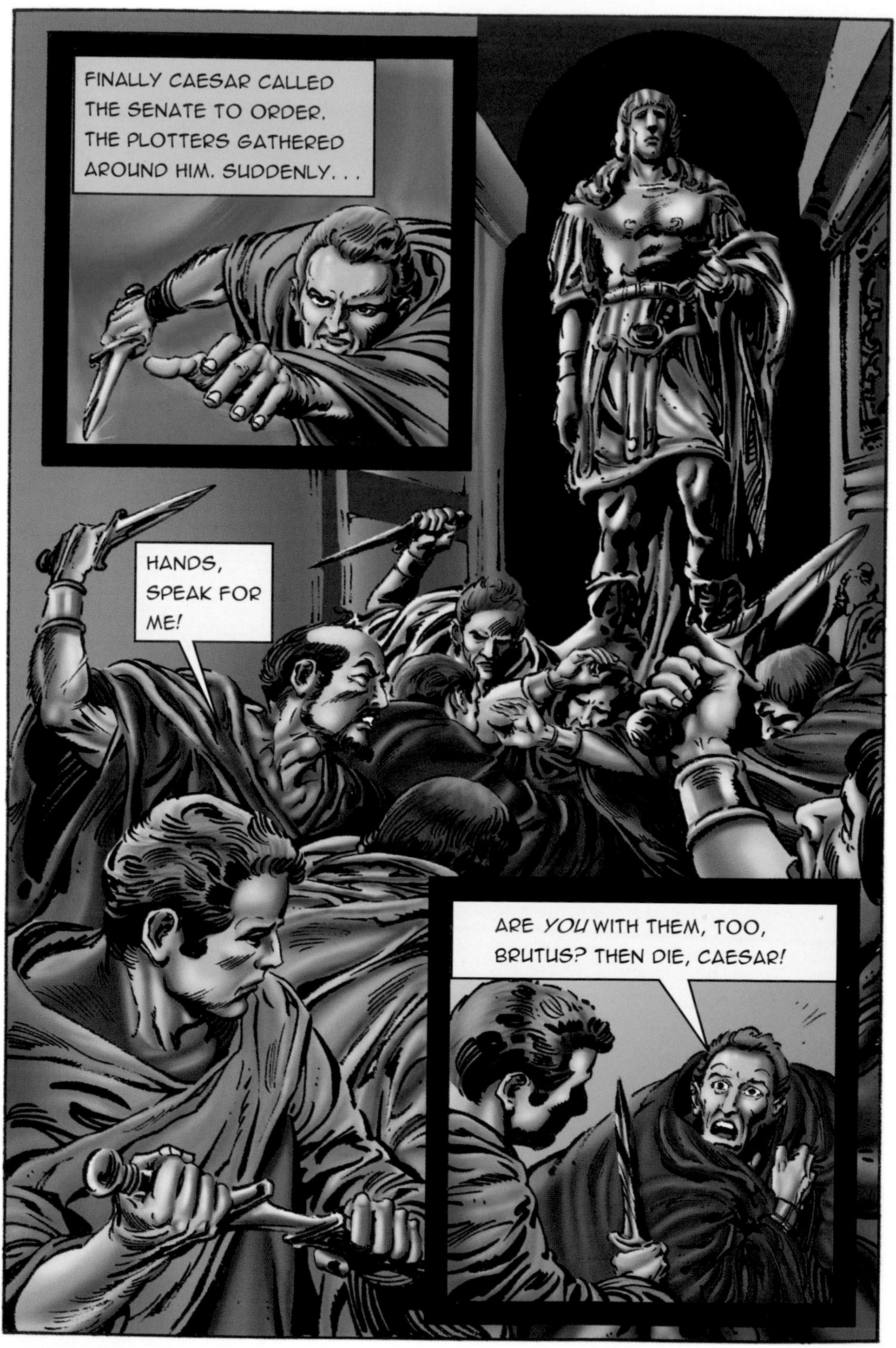
FINALLY CAESAR CALLED THE SENATE TO ORDER. THE PLOTTERS GATHERED AROUND HIM. SUDDENLY. . .
HANDS, SPEAK FOR ME!
ARE *YOU* WITH THEM, TOO, BRUTUS? THEN DIE, CAESAR!

AS CAESAR FELL, THE CROWD PANICKED,* BUT THE PLOTTERS CHEERED.

LIBERTY! FREEDOM! TYRANNY** IS DEAD!

TELL THE PEOPLE WE HAVE MADE THEM FREE AGAIN!

WE MEAN NO HARM TO ANY ROMAN! NO ONE SHOULD BE FRIGHTENED!

WHERE IS MARK ANTONY?

HE FLED TO HIS HOME. EVERYWHERE MEN, WOMEN, AND CHILDREN ARE CRYING AND RUNNING AWAY.

CAESAR'S DEATH WAS A *SACRIFICE*, NOT A MURDER. WE MUST BATHE OUR HANDS AND OUR SWORDS IN HIS BLOOD AND GO THROUGH THE STREETS CRYING, "PEACE, FREEDOM, AND LIBERTY!"

* became frightened and tried to run away all at once

** harsh rule

JUST THEN MARK ANTONY'S SERVANT DREW NEAR.

MY MASTER SENT ME TO KNEEL AT YOUR FEET, BRUTUS, WITH A MESSAGE.

THEN SPEAK.

"I HONOR BRUTUS," MY MASTER SAID, "AS I HONORED CAESAR."

IF YOU WILL MAKE CLEAR TO ANTONY WHY CAESAR DESERVED TO DIE, THEN HE WILL HONOR BRUTUS LIVING MORE THAN CAESAR DEAD. AND HE WILL FOLLOW YOU FAITHFULLY.

ANTONY IS A WISE AND BRAVE ROMAN! HE MAY SAFELY COME HERE, AND I WILL ANSWER ALL HIS QUESTIONS.

I'LL TELL HIM AT ONCE.

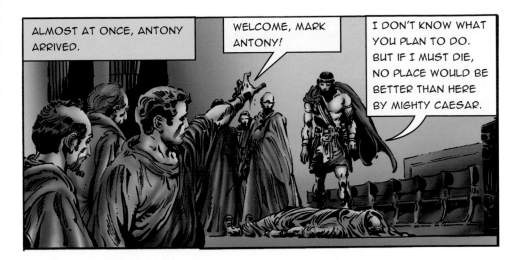

ALMOST AT ONCE, ANTONY ARRIVED.

WELCOME, MARK ANTONY!

I DON'T KNOW WHAT YOU PLAN TO DO. BUT IF I MUST DIE, NO PLACE WOULD BE BETTER THAN HERE BY MIGHTY CAESAR.

WE MAY SEEM CRUEL AND BLOODY TO YOU NOW, BUT OUR HEARTS ARE NOT. PITY FOR THE ROMAN PEOPLE MADE US DO WHAT WE DID.

WE WISH YOU WELL. AND WHEN WE HAVE CALMED THE FEARS OF THE PEOPLE, I WILL EXPLAIN WHY I, WHO HONORED CAESAR ALSO, STRUCK HIM DOWN.

VERY WELL. THEN I WOULD LIKE TO TAKE HIS BODY TO THE MARKETPLACE AND SPEAK AT HIS FUNERAL.*

YOU SHALL, MARK ANTONY.

BRUTUS, A WORD WITH YOU!

* a religious service for someone who has died

DON'T LET HIM SPEAK BRUTUS! HE'LL STIR UP THE PEOPLE!

DON'T WORRY, CASSIUS. I WILL SPEAK FIRST AND EXPLAIN EVERYTHING WE HAVE DONE.

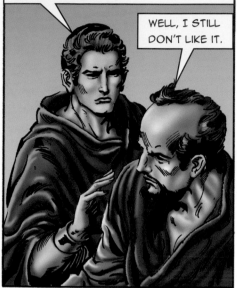

IT WILL DO US MORE GOOD THAN HARM TO SHOW THE PEOPLE THAT WE WANT TO HAVE A PROPER FUNERAL FOR CAESAR.

WELL, I STILL DON'T LIKE IT.

SO IT WAS ARRANGED. THE PLOTTERS WENT AWAY AND MARK ANTONY WAS LEFT ALONE WITH CAESAR'S BODY.

OH, CAESAR, FORGIVE ME FOR BEING MEEK AND GENTLE WITH THESE BUTCHERS. THEY HAVE KILLED THE NOBLEST MAN WHO EVER LIVED!

I SWEAR THAT BEFORE THIS IS OVER, I WILL AVENGE* YOU! BLOOD, SUFFERING, AND WAR WILL TEAR ITALY APART!

* get even for something, seek revenge

AS ANTONY GRIEVED* FOR CAESAR, A SERVANT CAME TO HIM FROM OCTAVIUS, CAESAR'S NEPHEW AND ADOPTED SON.

CAESAR WROTE TO YOUR MASTER, TELLING HIM TO RETURN TO ROME! IS HE NEAR?

ONLY A FEW MILES AWAY. BUT—IS THIS CAESAR?

IT IS. BUT BEFORE WE WEEP, WE MUST MAKE PLANS. RETURN TO OCTAVIUS AND TELL HIM WHAT HAS HAPPENED.

NOW COME, GIVE ME A HAND WITH CAESAR'S BODY.

WE MUST CARRY HIM TO THE MARKETPLACE. I WILL SEE FROM MY SPEECH HOW THE PEOPLE WILL ANSWER THIS MURDER!

*mourned, felt sorrow at someone's death

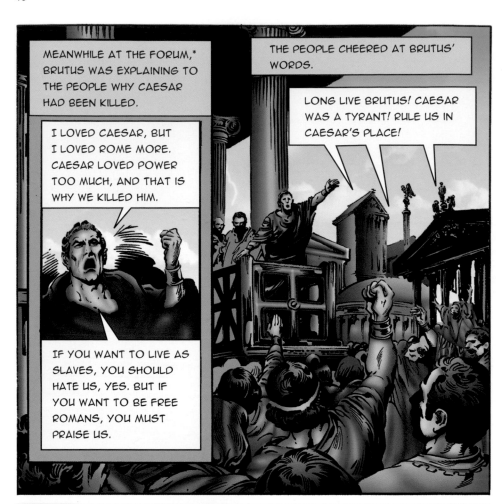

MEANWHILE AT THE FORUM,* BRUTUS WAS EXPLAINING TO THE PEOPLE WHY CAESAR HAD BEEN KILLED.

I LOVED CAESAR, BUT I LOVED ROME MORE. CAESAR LOVED POWER TOO MUCH, AND THAT IS WHY WE KILLED HIM.

IF YOU WANT TO LIVE AS SLAVES, YOU SHOULD HATE US, YES. BUT IF YOU WANT TO BE FREE ROMANS, YOU MUST PRAISE US.

THE PEOPLE CHEERED AT BRUTUS' WORDS.

LONG LIVE BRUTUS! CAESAR WAS A TYRANT! RULE US IN CAESAR'S PLACE!

JUST THEN MARK ANTONY ARRIVED WITH CAESAR'S BODY.

GOOD ROMANS, DO HONOR TO CAESAR'S BODY, AND LISTEN TO ANTONY'S FUNERAL SPEECH. I ALONE WILL LEAVE.

* a central meeting place in the city of Rome

SAYING THIS, BRUTUS DEPARTED, AND ANTONY BEGAN TO SPEAK.

THE NOBLE BRUTUS HAS TOLD YOU CAESAR WAS TOO AMBITIOUS*. . . AND BRUTUS IS AN HONORABLE MAN.

BUT THREE TIMES YOU SAW ME OFFER CAESAR A CROWN, AND THREE TIMES HE REFUSED IT. IS THIS *AMBITION*?

HE LOVED YOU VERY MUCH, AND YOU LOVED *HIM* ONCE, TOO, WITH GOOD REASON.

AS ANTONY RECALLED** CAESAR'S GREAT DEEDS, THE FEELINGS OF THE CROWD BEGAN TO CHANGE.

BUT WAIT—I'VE SAID TOO MUCH. I MUST NOT WRONG THE HONORABLE MEN WHO HAVE KILLED CAESAR.

THEY WERE MURDERERS! O NOBLE CAESAR!

* wanting or trying to get power

** reminded someone of

BE CALM, MY FRIENDS! LISTEN TO CAESAR'S WILL!

WE'LL HEAR IT! WE'LL HEAR THE WILL!

TO EVERY ROMAN MAN, HE LEAVES SEVENTY-FIVE DRACHMAS.*

TO YOU AND YOUR CHILDREN HE LEAVES HIS LANDS, WALKS, AND GARDENS ON THE RIVER TIBER. WHEN SHALL COME ANOTHER MAN LIKE THIS?

NEVER! NEVER!

MOST NOBLE CAESAR! WE'LL BURN HIS BODY IN THE HOLY PLACE! WE'LL AVENGE HIS DEATH!

* about $150

WE'LL FIND THE TRAITORS!* WE'LL BURN THEIR HOUSES! WE'LL KILL THEM!

NOW LET IT WORK. MISCHIEF** TAKE YOUR COURSE.

AS THE MOB MOVED AWAY, OCTAVIUS' SERVANT WALKED UP TO ANTONY.

OCTAVIUS IS IN ROME. . . AT CAESAR'S HOUSE.

I WILL GO STRAIGHT TO VISIT HIM.

THEY SAY BRUTUS AND CASSIUS HAVE RIDDEN LIKE MADMEN OUT OF ROME!

THEY MUST HAVE HAD SOME WARNING OF HOW THE PEOPLE FEEL.

* people who have done evil to their own country

** evil works, violence

ONCE CAESAR WAS DEAD, BRUTUS AND CASSIUS HAD HOPED TO TAKE CONTROL OF ROME PEACEFULLY. BUT ANTONY'S SPEECH CHANGED EVERYTHING. THEY WOULD HAVE TO FIGHT A BATTLE TO DECIDE WHICH SIDE WOULD RULE.

MARK ANTONY AND OCTAVIUS MADE THEIR PLANS IN ROME.

BRUTUS AND CAS- SIUS ARE RAISING ARMIES. WE MUST GET OUR OWN FORCES TOGETHER.

AND WE MUST TRY TO LEARN THEIR PLANS. THERE ARE ENEMIES ON ALL SIDES.

OUTSIDE ROME, BRUTUS AND CASSIUS COMMANDED A LARGE ARMY. THEY MET ONE DAY AT BRUTUS' CAMP.

I HAVE WORD THAT ANTONY AND OCTAVIUS ARE LEADING A STRONG FORCE TO PHILIPPI.

I HEAR THE SAME.

WE MUST MARCH THERE TO FIGHT THEM.

NO, NO! IT'S BETTER FOR THEM TO MARCH TO *US*, TIRING THEIR SOLDIERS!

NOT SO, FOR THEY CAN ADD NEW SOLDIERS TO THEIR ARMY AS THEY TRAVEL. THEY WILL BE *STRONGER* IF THEY COME HERE.

THEN WE WILL DO IT YOUR WAY. BUT I DON'T LIKE IT.

COME! IT IS NIGHT AND TIME FOR US TO REST.

YES. LET'S NOT ARGUE EVER AGAIN.

WHEN CASSIUS HAD LEFT, BRUTUS MADE READY FOR THE NIGHT.

IF YOU ARE NOT TOO SLEEPY LUCIUS, PLAY ME A TUNE.

IT IS MY DUTY, SIR.

LUCIUS PLAYED, AND NODDED, AND FELL ASLEEP.

THIS CANDLE BURNS BADLY. . . OR IS IT MY EYES? WHO COMES HERE?

WHAT ARE YOU? AN ANGEL? A DEVIL? YOU MAKE MY BLOOD FREEZE AND MY HAIR STAND ON END.

I AM YOUR EVIL SPIRIT, BRUTUS. YOU WILL SEE ME AGAIN. . . AT PHILIPPI!

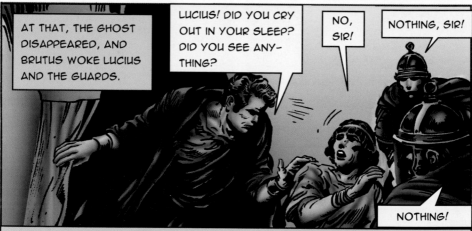

AT THAT, THE GHOST DISAPPEARED, AND BRUTUS WOKE LUCIUS AND THE GUARDS.

LUCIUS! DID YOU CRY OUT IN YOUR SLEEP? DID YOU SEE ANY-THING?

NO, SIR!

NOTHING, SIR!

NOTHING!

AFTER THIS, BRUTUS SPENT AN UNEASY NIGHT. THE NEXT DAY, ON THE PLAINS OF PHILIPPI, THE TWO ARMIES MET TO DO BATTLE.

OUR HOPES ARE ANSWERED! THEY'VE COME DOWN FROM THE HILLS TO FIGHT ON THE PLAINS.

THEY ARE COMING, AND THEIR FLAG IS OUT!

GOOD. OCTAVIUS, LEAD YOUR MEN AGAINST THE LEFT PART OF THE FIELD. I'LL TAKE THE RIGHT.

WORDS BEFORE BLOWS,* COUNTRYMEN.**

BUT BEFORE THE BATTLE BEGAN, THE LEADERS MET TO TALK.

YOU LOVE YOUR WORDS MORE THAN WE DO, BRUTUS.

BUT GOOD WORDS ARE BETTER THAN BAD BLOWS.

WITH YOUR BAD BLOWS YOU GIVE GOOD WORDS BRUTUS. . . LIKE THE HOLE YOU MADE IN CAESAR'S HEART WHILE CRYING, "LONG LIVE CAESAR!"

* hits, strikes (in a battle)

** fellow citizens

I DRAW MY SWORD AGAINST ALL PLOTTERS! IT WILL NOT BE PUT AWAY AGAIN UNTIL CAESAR'S WOUNDS ARE AVENGED. . . OR UNTIL *I* FALL IN BATTLE!

COME, ANTONY, WE CHALLENGE* YOU! IF YOU DARE TO FIGHT, MEET US ON THE BATTLEFIELD!

WITH THIS, ANTONY AND OCTAVIUS MOVED AWAY. BRUTUS SPOKE WITH HIS LIEUTENANT**, LUCILIUS; CASSIUS WITH HIS AIDE, MESSALA.

TODAY IS MY BIRTHDAY, MESSALA, AND THE SIGNS ARE BAD. I DO NOT LIKE TO STAKE EVERYTHING ON ONE BATTLE!

* dare

** the man next in charge

CASSIUS SPOKE OF THESE FEARS TO BRUTUS.

IF WE LOSE THIS BATTLE, WHAT THEN, BRUTUS? ARE YOU WILLING TO BE LED THROUGH THE STREETS OF ROME A CAPTIVE?*

NO, CASSIUS! BRUTUS WILL NEVER GO TO ROME IN CHAINS!

BUT THIS DAY MUST END WHAT THE IDES OF MARCH BEGAN. WHETHER WE SHALL EVER MEET AGAIN, WE DON'T KNOW!

FOREVER AND FOREVER FAREWELL, CASSIUS! IF WE *DO* MEET AGAIN, WHY, WE SHALL SMILE!

FOREVER AND FOREVER FAREWELL, BRUTUS! IF WE DO NOT, IT IS RIGHT THAT WE SAY OUR GOODBYES NOW!

* prisoner, loser of a battle

THE BATTLE WENT ON ALL DAY.

RIDE, MESSALA! GIVE THESE ORDERS TO THE TROOPS ACROSS THE FIELD.

I SEE A WEAKNESS IN OCTAVIUS' WING*. A SUDDEN ATTACK WILL BEAT THEM.

BUT ON ANOTHER PART OF THE BATTLEFIELD, THINGS WERE NOT GOING WELL FOR CASSIUS.

MY OWN MEN WERE RUNNING AWAY, TITINIUS. I HAD TO KILL THE FLAG BEARER AND TAKE THE FLAG FROM HIM!

BRUTUS GAVE THE COMMAND TO ATTACK OCTAVIUS TOO EARLY. WE ARE SURROUNDED** BY ANTONY'S MEN!

* a group of men in battle, part of an army

** hemmed in on all sides

JUST THEN, PINDARUS, ONE OF CASSIUS' MEN, RUSHED UP.

RETREAT,* SIR! GET AWAY! ANTONY HAS CAPTURED YOUR TENTS!

THOSE ARE *MY* TENTS BURNING?

THEY ARE, SIR.

TITINIUS. . . QUICK! RIDE OUT AND LEARN WHETHER THOSE NEARBY TROOPS ARE FRIENDS OR ENEMIES.

I'LL BE RIGHT BACK!

LOOK OUT OVER THE FIELD, PINDARUS! TELL ME WHAT IS HAPPENING!

TITINIUS IS RIDING TOWARD SOME HORSEMEN**. . . THEY SURROUND HIM. . . THEY SHOUT WITH JOY! THEY'VE *CAPTURED* HIM!

* go back

** in this case, soldiers on horseback

TITINIUS, MY DEAR FRIEND. . . I SENT HIM TO BE CAPTURED!

COME DOWN, PINDARUS. WHEN I SPARED YOUR LIFE* IN BATTLE, YOU SWORE TO DO WHATEVER I TOLD YOU. NOW DO WHAT I SAY, AND YOU WILL BE FREE.

TAKE THIS SWORD, THE SAME ONE THAT KILLED CAESAR. WHEN MY FACE IS COVERED, THRUST** IT DEEP INTO MY CHEST.

I WILL DO IT, BUT I WOULD RATHER NOT BE FREE IN SUCH A WAY!

SADLY, PINDARUS DID AS HE WAS ORDERED.

CAESAR, YOU ARE AVENGED!

* did not kill someone, kept someone from being killed

** push, strike

JUST THEN TITINIUS RETURNED WITH MESSALA. HE HAD NOT BEEN CAPTURED AFTER ALL!

SO FAR, THE BATTLE IS A DRAW.* CASSIUS' TROOPS WERE BEATEN BY ANTONY, BUT BRUTUS WON OUT OVER OCTAVIUS.

THAT WILL COMFORT, CASSIUS. I LEFT HIM HERE SOMEWHERE.

ISN'T THAT CASSIUS ON THE GROUND?

OH NO, MESSALA; THAT *WAS* CASSIUS! HE IS NO MORE.

I'LL TAKE THIS SAD NEWS TO BRUTUS.

CASSIUS MUST HAVE THOUGHT WE COULD NOT WIN!

OH, CASSIUS! YOU SENT ME OUT. . . I MET OUR FRIENDS. DIDN'T YOU HEAR THEIR SHOUTS? NO, YOU MISUNDERSTOOD EVERYTHING. . . YOU THOUGHT THEY WERE ENEMIES WHO CAPTURED ME!

* even on both sides

** did not understand, made a mistake

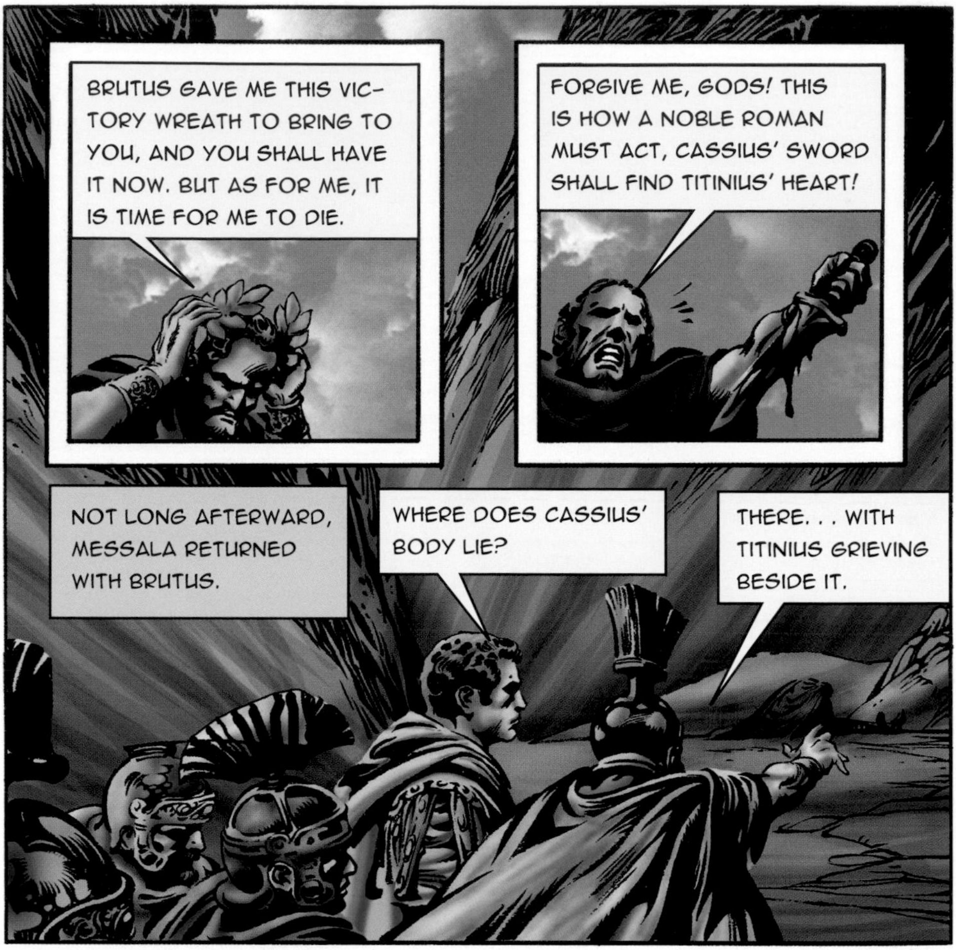
BRUTUS GAVE ME THIS VICTORY WREATH TO BRING TO YOU, AND YOU SHALL HAVE IT NOW. BUT AS FOR ME, IT IS TIME FOR ME TO DIE.
FORGIVE ME, GODS! THIS IS HOW A NOBLE ROMAN MUST ACT, CASSIUS' SWORD SHALL FIND TITINIUS' HEART!
NOT LONG AFTERWARD, MESSALA RETURNED WITH BRUTUS.
WHERE DOES CASSIUS' BODY LIE?
THERE. . . WITH TITINIUS GRIEVING BESIDE IT.

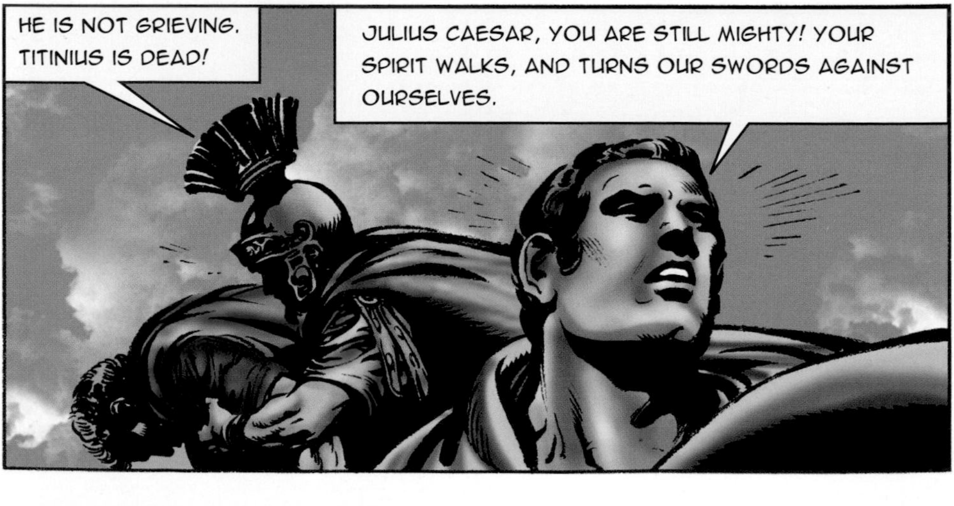
HE IS NOT GRIEVING. TITINIUS IS DEAD!
JULIUS CAESAR, YOU ARE STILL MIGHTY! YOUR SPIRIT WALKS, AND TURNS OUR SWORDS AGAINST OURSELVES.

FRIENDS, I OWE MORE TEARS TO THIS DEAD MAN THAN YOU SHALL SEE ME PAY.

FOR NOW, TAKE THE BODIES AWAY. THERE IS STILL A BATTLE TO BE FOUGHT.

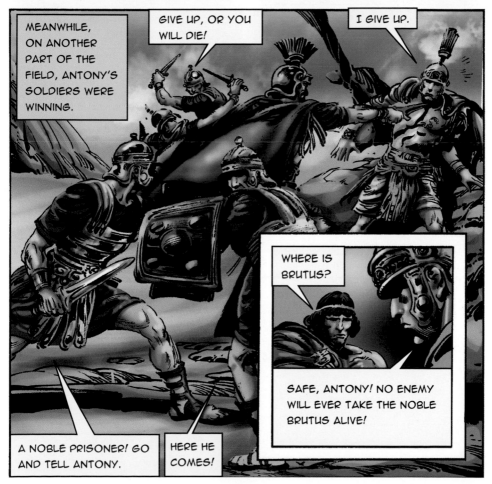

MEANWHILE, ON ANOTHER PART OF THE FIELD, ANTONY'S SOLDIERS WERE WINNING.

GIVE UP, OR YOU WILL DIE!

I GIVE UP.

WHERE IS BRUTUS?

SAFE, ANTONY! NO ENEMY WILL EVER TAKE THE NOBLE BRUTUS ALIVE!

A NOBLE PRISONER! GO AND TELL ANTONY.

HERE HE COMES!

AT THAT VERY MOMENT, NOT FAR AWAY, BRUTUS WAS BEGINNING TO SEE THAT HE COULD NOT WIN.

COME, MY FRIENDS. REST ON THIS ROCK.

LAST NIGHT CAESAR'S GHOST APPEARED* TO ME. I KNOW MY TIME HAS COME. WHO WILL HELP ME TO DIE?

CLITUS? DARDANIUS?

I, SIR? NOT FOR ALL THE WORLD!

I'D RATHER KILL MYSELF!

JUST THEN THE TRUMPETS SOUNDED. ENEMY TROOPS DREW NEAR.

RUN, SIR! QUICKLY!

YOU GO, AND I WILL FOLLOW. GOOD STRATO, STAY BY ME.

*as used here, came back from the dead as a spirit and revealed who he was

HOLD MY SWORD, AND TURN YOUR FACE AWAY WHILE I RUN UPON IT. WILL YOU, STRATO?

GIVE ME YOUR HAND, FIRST.

FARE YOU WELL, DEAR SIR!

FAREWELL, GOOD STRATO. CAESAR, YOU ARE AVENGED!

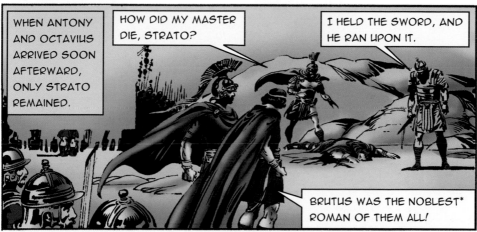

WHEN ANTONY AND OCTAVIUS ARRIVED SOON AFTERWARD, ONLY STRATO REMAINED.

HOW DID MY MASTER DIE, STRATO?

I HELD THE SWORD, AND HE RAN UPON IT.

BRUTUS WAS THE NOBLEST* ROMAN OF THEM ALL!

THE BATTLE WAS OVER, AND ANTONY'S SIDE HAD WON. BUT EVEN SO, HE WAS SAD AT BRUTUS' DEATH.

ALL THE OTHERS ACTED BE-CAUSE THEY ENVIED** CAESAR. BRUTUS ALONE DID WHAT HE BELIEVED WAS RIGHT!

HIS BODY SHALL LIE IN HONOR IN MY TENT. WE WILL GIVE HIM ALL THE RE-SPECT A NOBLE ROMAN SOLDIER DESERVES!

THE END

* best, most honest, most sincere

** were jealous of